Time Eno
By Lynn

The atomic bomb meant, to most people, the end. To Henry Bemis it meant something far different—a thing to appreciate and enjoy.

or a long time, Henry Bemis had had an ambition. To read a book. Not just the title or the preface, or a page somewhere in the middle. He wanted to read the whole thing, all the way through from beginning to end. A simple ambition perhaps, but in the cluttered life of Henry Bemis, an impossibility.

Henry had no time of his own. There was his wife, Agnes who owned that part of it that his employer, Mr. Carsville, did not buy. Henry was allowed enough to get to and from work—that in itself being quite a concession on Agnes' part.

Also, nature had conspired against Henry by handing him with a pair of hopelessly myopic eyes. Poor Henry literally couldn't see his hand in front of his face. For a while, when he was very young, his parents had thought him an idiot. When they realized it was his eyes, they got glasses for him. He was never quite able to catch up. There was never enough time. It looked as though Henry's ambition would never be realized. Then something happened which changed all that.

Henry was down in the vault of the Eastside Bank & Trust when it happened. He had stolen a few moments from the duties of his teller's cage to try to read a few pages of the magazine he had bought that morning. He'd made an excuse to Mr. Carsville about needing bills in large denominations for a certain customer, and then, safe inside the dim recesses of the vault he had pulled from inside his coat the pocket size magazine.

He had just started a picture article cheerfully entitled "The New Weapons and What They'll Do To YOU", when all the noise in the world crashed in upon his ear-drums. It seemed to be inside of him and outside of him all at once. Then the concrete floor was rising up at him and the ceiling came slanting down toward him, and for a fleeting second Henry thought of a story he had started to read once called "The Pit and The Pendulum". He regretted in that insane moment that he had never had time to finish that story to see how it came out. Then all was darkness and quiet and unconsciousness.

hen Henry came to, he knew that something was desperately wrong with the Eastside Bank & Trust. The heavy steel door of the vault was buckled and twisted and the floor tilted up at a dizzy angle, while the ceiling dipped crazily toward it. Henry gingerly got to his feet, moving arms and legs experimentally. Assured that nothing was broken, he tenderly raised a hand to his eyes. His precious glasses were intact, thank God! He would never have been able to find his way out of the shattered vault without them.

He made a mental note to write Dr. Torrance to have a spare pair made and mailed to him. Blasted nuisance not having his prescription on file locally, but Henry trusted no-one but Dr. Torrance to grind those thick lenses into his own complicated prescription. Henry removed the heavy glasses from his face. Instantly the room dissolved into a neutral blur. Henry saw a pink splash that he knew was his hand, and a white blob come up to meet the pink as he withdrew his pocket handkerchief and carefully dusted the lenses. As he replaced the glasses, they slipped down on the bridge of his nose a little. He had been meaning to have them tightened for some time.

He suddenly realized, without the realization actually entering his conscious thoughts, that something momentous had happened, something worse than the boiler blowing up, something worse than a gas main exploding, something worse than anything that had ever happened before. He felt that way because it was so quiet. There was no whine of sirens, no shouting, no running, just an ominous and all pervading silence.

enry walked across the slanting floor. Slipping and stumbling on the uneven surface, he made his way to the elevator. The car lay crumpled at the foot of the shaft like a discarded accordian. There was something inside of it that Henry could not look at, something that had once been a person, or perhaps several people, it was impossible to tell now.

Feeling sick, Henry staggered toward the stairway. The steps were still there, but so jumbled and piled back upon one another that it was more like climbing the side of a mountain than mounting a stairway. It was quiet in the huge chamber that had been the lobby of the bank. It looked strangely cheerful with the sunlight shining through the girders where the ceiling had fallen. The dappled sunlight glinted across the silent lobby, and everywhere there were huddled lumps of unpleasantness that made Henry sick as he tried not to look at them.

"Mr. Carsville," he called. It was very quiet. Something had to be done, of course. This was terrible, right in the middle of a Monday, too. Mr. Carsville would know what to do. He called again, more loudly, and his voice cracked hoarsely, "Mr. Carrrrsville!" And then he saw an arm and shoulder extending out from under a huge fallen block of marble ceiling. In the buttonhole was the white carnation Mr. Carsville had worn to work that morning, and on the third finger of that hand was a massive signet ring, also belonging to Mr. Carsville. Numbly, Henry realized that the rest of Mr. Carsville was under that block of marble.

Henry felt a pang of real sorrow. Mr. Carsville was gone,

and so was the rest of the staff—Mr. Wilkinson and Mr. Emory and Mr. Prithard, and the same with Pete and Ralph and Jenkins and Hunter and Pat the guard and Willie the doorman. There was no one to say what was to be done about the Eastside Bank & Trust except Henry Bemis, and Henry wasn't worried about the bank, there was something he wanted to do.

He climbed carefully over piles of fallen masonry. Once he stepped down into something that crunched and squashed beneath his feet and he set his teeth on edge to keep from retching. The street was not much different from the inside, bright sunlight and so much concrete to crawl over, but the unpleasantness was much, much worse. Everywhere there were strange, motionless lumps that Henry could not look at.

Suddenly, he remembered Agnes. He should be trying to get to Agnes, shouldn't he? He remembered a poster he had seen that said, "In event of emergency do not use the telephone, your loved ones are as safe as you." He wondered about Agnes. He looked at the smashed automobiles, some with their four wheels pointing skyward like the stiffened legs of dead animals. He couldn't get to Agnes now anyway, if she was safe, then, she was safe, otherwise ... of course, Henry knew Agnes wasn't safe. He had a feeling that there wasn't anyone safe for a long, long way, maybe not in the whole state or the whole country, or the whole world. No, that was a thought Henry didn't want to think, he forced it from his mind and turned his thoughts back to Agnes.

he had been a pretty good wife, now that it was all said and done. It wasn't exactly her fault if people didn't have time to read nowadays. It was just that there was the house, and the bank, and the yard. There were the Jones' for bridge and the Graysons' for canasta and charades with the Bryants. And the television, the television Agnes loved to watch, but would never watch alone. He never had time to read even a newspaper. He started thinking about last night, that business about the newspaper.

Henry had settled into his chair, quietly, afraid that a creaking spring might call to Agnes' attention the fact that he was momentarily unoccupied. He had unfolded the newspaper slowly and carefully, the sharp crackle of the paper would have been a clarion call to Agnes. He had glanced at the headlines of the first page. "Collapse Of

Conference Imminent." He didn't have time to read the article. He turned to the second page. "Solon Predicts War Only Days Away." He flipped through the pages faster, reading brief snatches here and there, afraid to spend too much time on any one item. On a back page was a brief article entitled, "Prehistoric Artifacts Unearthed In Yucatan". Henry smiled to himself and carefully folded the sheet of paper into fourths. That would be interesting, he would read all of it. Then it came, Agnes' voice. "Henrrreee!" And then she was upon him. She lightly flicked the paper out of his hands and into the fireplace. He saw the flames lick up and curl possessively around the unread article. Agnes continued, "Henry, tonight is the Jones' bridge night. They'll be here in thirty minutes and I'm not dressed yet, and here you are ... *reading*." She had emphasized the last word as though it were an unclean act. "Hurry and shave, you know how smooth Jasper Jones' chin always looks, and then straighten up this room." She glanced regretfully toward the fireplace. "Oh dear, that paper, the television schedule ... oh well, after the Jones leave there won't be time for anything but the late-late movie and.... Don't just sit there, Henry, hurrreeee!"

Henry was hurrying now, but hurrying too much. He cut his leg on a twisted piece of metal that had once been an automobile fender. He thought about things like lock-jaw and gangrene and his hand trembled as he tied his pocket-handkerchief around the wound. In his mind, he saw the fire again, licking across the face of last night's newspaper. He thought that now he would have time to read all the newspapers he wanted to, only now there wouldn't be any more. That heap of rubble across the street had been the Gazette Building. It was terrible to think there would never be another up to date newspaper. Agnes would have been very upset, no television schedule. But then, of course, no television. He wanted to laugh but he didn't. That wouldn't have been fitting, not at all.

He could see the building he was looking for now, but the silhouette was strangely changed. The great circular dome was now a ragged semi-circle, half of it gone, and one of the great wings of the building had fallen in upon itself. A sudden panic gripped Henry Bemis. What if they were all ruined, destroyed, every one of them? What if there wasn't a single one left? Tears of helplessness welled in his eyes as he painfully fought his way over and through the twisted fragments of the city.

e thought of the building when it had been whole. He remembered the many nights he had paused outside its wide and welcoming doors. He thought of the warm nights when the doors had been thrown open and he could see the people inside, see them sitting at the plain wooden tables with the stacks of books beside them. He used to think then, what a wonderful thing a public library was, a place where anybody, anybody at all could go in and read.

He had been tempted to enter many times. He had watched the people through the open doors, the man in greasy work clothes who sat near the door, night after night, laboriously studying, a technical journal perhaps, difficult for him, but promising a brighter future. There had been an aged, scholarly gentleman who sat on the other side of the door, leisurely paging, moving his lips a little as he did so, a man having little time left, but rich in time because he could do with it as he chose.

Henry had never gone in. He had started up the steps once, got almost to the door, but then he remembered Agnes, her questions and shouting, and he had turned away.

He was going in now though, almost crawling, his breath coming in stabbing gasps, his hands torn and bleeding. His trouser leg was sticky red where the wound in his leg had soaked through the handkerchief. It was throbbing badly but Henry didn't care. He had reached his destination.

Part of the inscription was still there, over the now doorless entrance. P-U-B—C L-I-B-R—. The rest had been torn away. The place was in shambles. The shelves were overturned, broken, smashed, tilted, their precious contents spilled in disorder upon the floor. A lot of the books, Henry noted gleefully, were still intact, still whole, still readable. He was literally knee deep in them, he wallowed in books. He picked one up. The title was "Collected Works of William Shakespeare." Yes, he must read that, sometime. He laid it aside carefully. He picked up another. Spinoza. He tossed it away, seized another, and another, and still another. Which to read first ... there were so many.

He had been conducting himself a little like a starving man in a delicatessen—grabbing a little of this and a little of that in a frenzy of enjoyment.

But now he steadied away. From the pile about him, he selected one volume, sat comfortably down on an overturned shelf, and opened the book.

Henry Bemis smiled.

There was the rumble of complaining stone. Minute in comparison which the epic complaints following the fall of the bomb. This one occurred under one corner of the shelf upon which Henry sat. The shelf moved; threw him off balance. The glasses slipped from his nose and fell with a tinkle.

He bent down, clawing blindly and found, finally, their smashed remains. A minor, indirect destruction stemming from the sudden, wholesale smashing of a city. But the only one that greatly interested Henry Bemis.

He stared down at the blurred page before him.

He began to cry.

——**THE END**——